Ricky Ricotta's Giant Robot

An Adventure Novel by
DAV PILKEY

Pictures by
MARTIN ONTIVEROS

THE BLUE SKY PRESS
An Imprint of Scholastic Inc. • New York

For Walter Bain Wills — D. P.

To my mom and my family, to all of my friends everywhere
(you know who you are), for their love and support,
and most of all to Micki, and our two kitties,
Bunny and Spanky — M. O.

THE BLUE SKY PRESS

Text copyright © 2000 by Dav Pilkey
Illustrations copyright © 2000 by Martin Ontiveros
All rights reserved.
No part of this publication may be reproduced
or stored in a retrieval system or transmitted
in any form or by any means, electronic,
mechanical, photocopying, recording, or otherwise,
without written permission of the publisher.
For information regarding permission,
please write to: Permissions Department,
The Blue Sky Press, an imprint of Scholastic Inc.,
555 Broadway, New York, New York 10012.
The Blue Sky Press is a registered trademark of Scholastic Inc.
Library of Congress catalog card number: 99-26548
ISBN 0-590-30719-3
10 9 8 7 6 5 4 3 2   0/0 01 02 03 04
Printed in the United States of America   37
First printing, February 2000

Chapters

CHAPTER 1

Ricky

There once was a mouse
named Ricky Ricotta who
lived in Squeakyville with
his mother and father.

5

Ricky liked living with
his mother and father, but
sometimes he got lonely.

Ricky wished he had a friend
to keep him company.

"Don't worry," said Ricky's father.
"Some day something **BIG** will
happen, and you will find a friend."
So Ricky waited.

CHAPTER 2

The Bullies

Ricky liked school, but he did not like walking to school. This was because Ricky was very small, and sometimes bullies picked on him.

"Where do you think you are going?" asked one of the bullies.

Ricky did not answer. He
turned and started to run.

The bullies chased him.

They knocked Ricky down
and threw his backpack
into a garbage can.

Every day, the bullies chased Ricky.
Every day, they knocked him down.
And every day, Ricky wished that
something **BIG** would happen.

14

CHAPTER 3

Dr. Stinky McNasty

That day at school, Ricky
ate lunch by himself. Then
he went outside for recess.

He watched the other mice
play a game of kickball.
Ricky did not know that
something **BIG** was about
to happen, but it *was*!

In a secret cave above
the city, a mad doctor was
planning something evil.

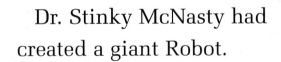

Dr. Stinky McNasty had
created a giant Robot.

"I will use this Robot to destroy the city," said Dr. Stinky, "and soon, I will rule the world!"

Dr. Stinky led his giant Robot into town.

"Robot," said Dr. Stinky, "I want you to **jump** and **stomp** and *destroy this city*!"

O-RAMA

HERE'S HOW IT WORKS!

STEP 1
Place your *left* hand inside the dotted lines marked "LEFT HAND HERE." Hold the book open *flat*.

STEP 2
Grasp the *right-hand* page with your right thumb and index finger (inside the dotted lines marked "RIGHT THUMB HERE").

STEP 3
Now *quickly* flip the right-hand page back and forth until the picture appears to be *animated*.

(For extra fun, try adding your own sound-effects!)

FLIP-O-RAMA 1

(pages 25 and 27)

Remember, flip *only* page 25.
While you are flipping, be sure
you can see the picture on page 25
and the one on page 27.
If you flip quickly, the two
pictures will start to look like
<u>one</u> *animated* picture.

Don't forget to add
your own sound-effects!

LEFT HAND HERE

The Robot Jumped.

RIGHT
THUMB
HERE

RIGHT
INDEX
FINGER
HERE

26

The Robot Jumped.

FLIP-O-RAMA 2

(pages 29 and 31)

Remember, flip *only* page 29.
While you are flipping, be sure
you can see the picture on page 29
and the one on page 31.
If you flip quickly, the two
pictures will start to look like
<u>one</u> *animated* picture.

Don't forget to add
your own sound-effects!

LEFT HAND HERE

The Robot Stomped.

RIGHT
INDEX
FINGER
HERE

30

The Robot Stomped.

FLIP-O-RAMA 3

(pages 33 and 35)

Remember, flip *only* page 33.
While you are flipping, be sure
you can see the picture on page 33
and the one on page 35.
If you flip quickly, the two
pictures will start to look like
<u>one</u> *animated* picture.

Don't forget to add
your own sound-effects!

LEFT HAND HERE

But the Robot Would Not Destroy the City.

RIGHT THUMB HERE

RIGHT
INDEX
FINGER
HERE

34

But the Robot Would Not Destroy the City.

CHAPTER 5

Ricky to the Rescue

Dr. Stinky was very angry.
"Destroy Squeakyville!" he
cried. "Destroy Squeakyville!"
But the Robot refused.

"I will teach you a lesson,"
said Dr. Stinky. He pressed
a button on his remote control
and zapped the Robot with
a terrible shock.

Ricky was watching.

"Stop it!" Ricky cried. But Dr.
Stinky kept on zapping the Robot.
Finally, Ricky aimed a kickball
at the evil doctor. Ricky kicked
as hard as he could.

"BOING!"

The kickball bounced
off Dr. Stinky's head. Dr.
Stinky dropped the controller,
and it broke on the ground.

"Rats! Rats! *RATS!*" cried Dr. Stinky. "I shall return!" And he disappeared down a sewer drain.

When the Robot saw what Ricky
had done, he walked over to Ricky.
Everyone screamed and ran.

But Ricky was not afraid. The Robot smiled and patted Ricky on the head.

Something **BIG** had happened after all!

CHAPTER 6
Ricky's Pet Robot

That afternoon, the Robot followed Ricky home from school.

Soon they got to Ricky's
house. "Wait here, Robot," said
Ricky. Ricky went inside.

"Mom, Dad," said Ricky, "can I have a pet?"

"Well," said Ricky's father, "you've been a good mouse lately."

"Yes," said Ricky's mother, "I think a pet would be good for you."

"Hooray!" said Ricky.
"Uh-oh," said Ricky's parents.

CHAPTER 7

Ricky's Giant Robot Helps Out

When Ricky's parents saw Ricky's new pet, they were not happy.

"That Robot is too big to be a pet," said Ricky's father.

"There is no room for him in our home," said Ricky's mom.

"But he is my friend,"
said Ricky, "and he will
help us around the house!"

Ricky's giant Robot used his super breath to blow all the leaves out of their yard. Ricky's dad liked that.

Ricky's Robot scared all the crows
out of the vegetable garden.
Ricky's mom liked that.

And when burglars drove
by the Ricottas' house,
they kept right on driving.
Everybody liked that!

"Well," said Ricky's father,
"I guess your Robot can live
in the garage."

"Hooray!" said Ricky.

CHAPTER 8

Back to School

The next day, Ricky and his Robot walked to school. The bullies were waiting for Ricky.

"Where do you think you're going?" asked one of the bullies.

"My Robot and I are going to school," said Ricky. The bullies looked up and saw Ricky's giant Robot. They were very frightened.

"Um…um…um…," said one
of the bullies, "can we carry
your backpack for you, sir?"

"Sure," said Ricky.

The bullies helped Ricky get to
school safely.

"Is there anything else we can
do for you, sir?" asked the bullies.

"No, thank you," said Ricky.

CHAPTER 9
Show-and-Tell

That day at school, Ricky's
class had show-and-tell. One
mouse brought a baseball
glove. Another mouse
brought a teddy bear.

Ricky brought his giant Robot.

Ricky's class got a free
ride on the Robot's back.

They flew up above the city
and over the mountains.

"This is fun!" said Ricky.

CHAPTER 10

Dr. Stinky's Revenge

While Ricky's class was flying
around in the sky, Dr. Stinky
sneaked over to the school.
He wanted revenge!

Dr. Stinky crept into Ricky's
classroom. He saw their pet lizard.
"This is just what I need!" said
Dr. Stinky.

He took out a bottle of Hate
Potion #9 and put a drop
into the lizard's water dish.
The lizard drank the water.

Suddenly, the lizard began to
grow and change. He got bigger and
bigger. He got meaner and meaner.

Soon, the lizard turned into
an evil monster.

"Destroy Ricky and his Robot!"
said Dr. Stinky.

"Yes, Master!" said the monster.

When Ricky's Robot saw
the evil monster, he flew down
to the schoolyard. Ricky and
his class climbed off quickly.
Then, the Robot turned toward
the giant monster, and the
battle began.

CHAPTER 11

The Big Battle

(IN FLIP-O-RAMA™)

FLIP-O-RAMA 4

(pages 73 and 75)

Remember, flip *only* page 73.
While you are flipping, be sure
you can see the picture on page 73
and the one on page 75.
If you flip quickly, the two
pictures will start to look like
<u>one</u> *animated* picture.

Don't forget to add
your own sound-effects!

LEFT HAND HERE

The Monster
Attacked.

RIGHT
THUMB
HERE

The Monster
Attacked.

FLIP-O-RAMA 5

(pages 77 and 79)

Remember, flip *only* page 77.
While you are flipping, be sure
you can see the picture on page 77
and the one on page 79.
If you flip quickly, the two
pictures will start to look like
<u>one</u> *animated* picture.

Don't forget to add
your own sound-effects!

LEFT HAND HERE

Ricky's Robot
Fought Back.

RIGHT
THUMB
HERE

RIGHT
INDEX
FINGER
HERE

78

Ricky's Robot
Fought Back.

FLIP-O-RAMA 6

(pages 81 and 83)

Remember, flip *only* page 81.
While you are flipping, be sure
you can see the picture on page 81
and the one on page 83.
If you flip quickly, the two
pictures will start to look like
<u>one</u> *animated* picture.

Don't forget to add
your own sound-effects!

LEFT HAND HERE

The Monster
Battled Hard.

RIGHT
THUMB
HERE

The Monster
Battled Hard.

FLIP-O-RAMA 7

(pages 85 and 87)

Remember, flip *only* page 85.
While you are flipping, be sure
you can see the picture on page 85
and the one on page 87.
If you flip quickly, the two
pictures will start to look like
<u>one</u> *animated* picture.

Don't forget to add
your own sound-effects!

LEFT HAND HERE

Ricky's Robot
Battled Harder.

RIGHT THUMB HERE

RIGHT
INDEX
FINGER
HERE

86

Ricky's Robot
Battled Harder.

FLIP-O-RAMA 8

(pages 89 and 91)

Remember, flip *only* page 89.
While you are flipping, be sure
you can see the picture on page 89
and the one on page 91.
If you flip quickly, the two
pictures will start to look like
<u>one</u> *animated* picture.

Don't forget to add
your own sound-effects!

LEFT HAND HERE

Ricky's Robot
Saved the Day.

RIGHT
THUMB
HERE

RIGHT
INDEX
FINGER
HERE

90

Ricky's Robot
Saved the Day.

CHAPTER 12

The Electro-Rocket

The monster was defeated, and all of his evil powers went away. Soon, he turned back into a tiny lizard and never bothered anybody again.

"Rats! Rats! *RATS!*" cried Dr. Stinky. "I will destroy that Robot myself!" He took his Electro-Rocket and aimed it at Ricky's Robot.

"NO!" screamed Ricky. He leaped onto Dr. Stinky just as the evil doctor fired his rocket.

Up, up, up went the rocket.
Ricky's Robot flew after it.
But he was not fast enough.

The rocket came down
and exploded.

"Ka-BOOM!" Right on
Dr. Stinky's secret cave.

CHAPTER 13

Justice Prevails

"Rats! Rats! *RATS!*" cried
Dr. Stinky. "This has been
a bad day for me!"

"It is about to get worse,"
said Ricky.

Ricky's giant Robot picked
up Dr. Stinky and put him
in the city jail.

CHAPTER 14

Back Home

That night, the Ricotta family
had a cookout in the backyard.
Ricky told his mom and dad all
about their adventures that day.

"Thank you for saving the city," said Ricky's father.

"And thank you for saving each other," said Ricky's mother.

"No problem," said Ricky…

..."that's what friends are for."

HOW TO DRAW RICKY'S ROBOT

1.
2.
3.
4.
5.
6.

1.

2.

3.

4.

5.

6.

HOW TO DRAW THE MONSTER

About the Author and Illustrator

DAV PILKEY created his first stories as comic books while he was in elementary school. In 1997, he wrote and illustrated his first adventure novel for children, *The Adventures of Captain Underpants*, which received rave reviews and was an instant bestseller—as were the three books that followed in the series. Dav is also the creator of numerous award-winning picture books, including *The Paperboy*, a Caldecott Honor Book, and the Dumb Bunnies books. He and his dog live in Seattle, Washington.

It was a stroke of luck when Dav discovered the work of artist **MARTIN ONTIVEROS**. Dav knew that Martin was just the right illustrator for the Ricky Ricotta's Giant Robot series. Martin lives in Portland, Oregon. He has a lot of toys as well as two cats, Bunny and Spanky.

COMING SOON:

Ricky Ricotta's Giant Robot

vs.

The Mutant Mosquitoes from Mercury

The Voodoo Vultures from Venus

The Mecha-Monkeys from Mars

The Jurassic Jack Rabbits from Jupiter

The Stupid Stinkbugs from Saturn

The Uranium Unicorns from Uranus

The Naughty Night Crawlers from Neptune

The Un-Pleasant Penguins from Pluto